Weird and Wonderful Trees

Jill McDougall

Contents

What Is a Tree?

This is my book about trees.

A tree is a kind of plant.
It has a woody stem, called a trunk.

There are all kinds of trees.

Some trees are tiny.
They can fit in your hand.

Some trees are HUGE!
They can make you feel small.

That's SO weird!

Parts of a Tree

A tree has different parts.

It has roots, a trunk, branches and leaves.

Each part has a job to do.

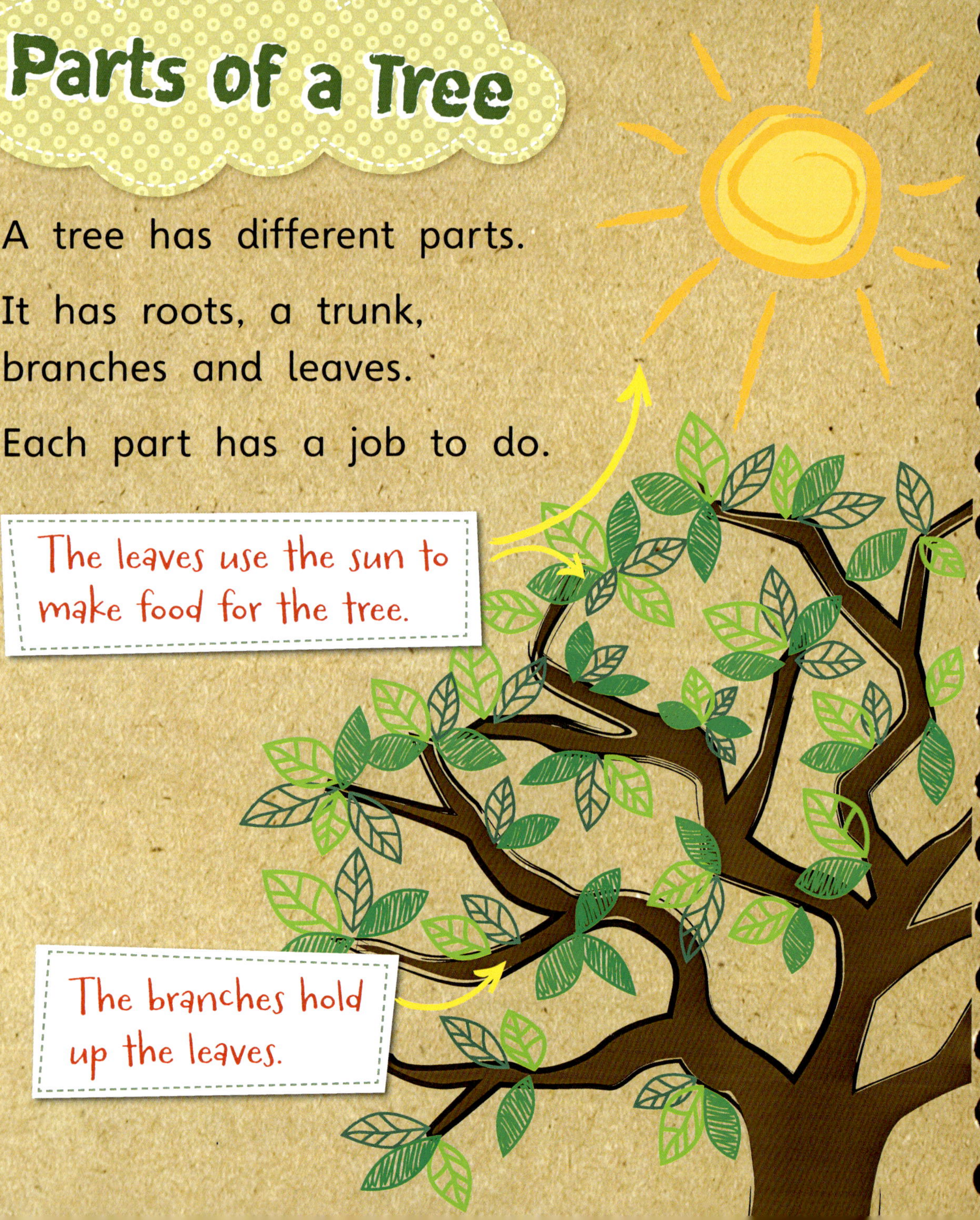

The leaves use the sun to make food for the tree.

The branches hold up the leaves.

The trunk lifts the branches and leaves up towards the sun.
The trunk carries water and food from the roots to the leaves.
The trunk carries food made by the leaves to the roots.
The roots take water and food from the soil.

Trunks

Weird and wonderful!

This is a redwood tree.
It is very tall and its trunk is HUGE!
Redwood trees are the biggest trees in the world.

A redwood tree can live for 2000 years.
That's a long time!

A hole has been cut in the trunk of this tree so cars can drive through it.

This tree is
96 metres tall!

This is a bottle tree.
Bottle trees grow in dry places.

They hold water in their trunk,
just like a bottle.
What a neat trick!

You can eat the leaves, seeds
and roots of a bottle tree.

There is water in here.

Roots

Weird and wonderful!

This is a pine tree.
Pine trees grow in dry places.

This tree has grown long roots.
They grow out from the tree.

The roots have tiny hairs on them.
The hairs soak up water for the tree.

The roots grow into the soil to stop the tree falling over.

This is a mangrove tree.
Mangrove trees grow in salty water.

They have thick leaves to keep out the salt.

Salt is not good for trees.
The roots lift the tree up
out of the salty water.

The roots of a mangrove tree
make a good home for little fish.

The roots look like stilts!

Leaves

Weird and wonderful!

This is a cocoa tree.
Cocoa trees grow in rainy places.

Too much rain is not good for leaves.
The cocoa tree has shiny leaves and
special tips to help the rain slide off.

Cocoa trees also have fruit.
The fruit can be made
into chocolate ... yum!

I think trees are weird and wonderful! Do you?

Picture Index